Calum Kerr is a short story and flash-fiction writer living in Southampton. He is an associate lecturer in Creative Writing at the University of Winchester, the fiction editor of Gumbo Press who produce the bi-monthly literary e-magazine, *Word Gumbo*, and is the Director for National Flash-Fiction Day 2012. His stories have appeared in a number of journals and magazines and his current project, *flash365*, can be viewed online at flash365.blogspot.com. More information can be found at www.calumkerr.co.uk.

Please note: all the following stories originally appeared in draft form on *flash365* during November 2011.

Braking Distance

by

CALUM KERR

SALT

LONDON

PUBLISHED BY SALT PUBLISHING
Acre House, 11–15 William Road, London NW1 3ER, United Kingdom

Salt Publishing 2012

Printed and bound in the United Kingdom by Lightning Source UK Ltd

Typeset in Bembo 12 / 13.5

ISBN 978 1 84471 912 9 paperback

1 3 5 7 9 8 6 4 2

Contents

Two Households, Both Alike

ROWAN WAS COUNTING DOWN the minutes until he could take his break. He always took it at the same time – 5.30 – and he always did the same thing. He would leave the Burger King concession by the door into the main corridor then head across the foyer to the main doors and across the car park to the smoking shelter near the car wash. He would get there and he would wait.

Rowan didn't smoke, but this was his daily pilgrimage.

And, every day, at 5.40, Julie would take her break. She would leave the KFC concession at the rear, walk down the service passage, exit from the side door, and head over to the same shelter.

Julie didn't smoke, but this was her daily pilgrimage.

Neither had ever been warned about fraternising with the enemy, but each knew from the comments of colleagues that theirs was an illicit liaison.

If other people were there, they would stand apart, make comments about getting some air somewhere sheltered, and separately head back in.

If they were alone, they would cling to each other, aware of the shortness of their time together, their lips locking over and over, their hands clutching and clasping, trying to make permanent the transient feel of body against body.

Their break was the only time they could be together. At the end of the shift, Julie's father would be waiting to pick her up and safely chaperone her home: a place which lay ten miles in the wrong direction for the car-less Rowan.

Their break was their only time, and it was infinitely precious.

Rowan watched as the clock ticked over from 5.29 to 5.30. He pulled the fryer out of the fat and hooked it up for the chips to drain, then he nodded to Maggie, who nodded back, and he headed for the door.

As he crossed in front of the cafeteria he heard a smash and a shout. He looked up in time for his eye to be caught by Barbara.

"Oh, Rowan, love, could you be a sweetie and get a mop for us quickly?" she called.

Rowan looked past her and saw Julie's back disappearing through the rear door of KFC, unaware of his problem, and then let his head drop in a nod.

"No worries, Barbara. I'll be right back." And he turned to fetch the mop, bucket and 'wet floor' sign thinking, *tomorrow and tomorrow and tomorrow.*

Take a Break

I ALWAYS STOP HERE whenever I'm on a long journey. There are plenty of other services I could visit, but this is the one I always choose. I can never work out exactly why.

Maybe it's the mix of people, after all the central location makes it a crossing point for many different journeys. Maybe it's the cosy warmth of it. Unlike other places the ceiling is relatively low, the lighting isn't too harsh and it's always a good temperature. Maybe it's the staff, they're always friendly but never over-inquisitive or prying.

Of course it could be that it's the same level of gravity as back home and the local hominids look similar enough that I can easily blend in.

This time I'm heading back from Ursa Minor to Aldebaran, mission completed. It's one of my regular routes. It always brings me past Earth and I always stop just here.

Ah, yes, I remember now why I choose this place. The car park is big enough for me to land easily. Strange how no-one ever seems to notice that my car comes down out of the sky rather than up off the slip road. That said, it's strange that they never notice that it's a spaceship rather than a car. Still, one of the things I've learned about service stations the galaxy over is that no-one wants to pay too much attention to anyone or anything. It's a place of transition, of transformation, and of hiatus. It's not a place that you would want to get caught up in anything.

Take the woman who ran past me when I came in. She was, oh, about twenty-five in earth years, I'd reckon. She was wearing a thick flannel shirt, leather work trousers, stout boots and carrying a vintage pistol. She pushed past me and into the cafeteria knocking a tray full of tea out of some man's hand, and then she ran out through the fire-exit and into the night. No-one really seemed to notice her, they were too intent on the fallen tray.

They didn't notice the man in the black cape who followed her either.

I guess, in the end, I come here because I feel at home. In a service station, everyone's a visitor, everyone's an alien, everyone's simply passing through.

Virtuous Patience

IT'S NOT ABOUT PLANNING, it's not about luck, it's about patience.

What am I talking about?

Everything, of course: everything good that ever happened to you in your life.

And patience isn't just about slogging along your chosen path or career, working doggedly at something until you get it right. I'm not talking about practise, for God's sake! No, it's just about being willing to put up with living one day after the next after the next. It's about getting up in the morning and putting on your smile, and eating all the shit that life gives you, until finally you get a little reward.

It's about living and waiting and never ever giving up.

It's about just being.

Oh, and keeping your eyes open.

It's about being in the services when some fool drops a tray. It's having the presence of mind not to stand and look, but to reach over and dip into the coat pockets hanging on the backs of the chairs in front of you.

It's about finding a wallet bulging with a little over £10,000 in wrinkled £50 notes. It's about calmly walking out, stepping over the expanding puddle of tea, and not looking shifty.

It's about waiting your turn and getting your reward. Yes, that's the secret of life.

Routine

Feed the twenty pound note into the machine. Take the pound coins from the slot.

Feed them all into the other machine.

Press the buttons, watch the reels, follow the lights, scoop up the winnings.

Feed them all into the machine.

Press the buttons, watch the reels, follow the lights, scoop up the winnings.

Feed them all into the machine.

Press the buttons, watch the reels, follow the lights, scoop up the winnings.

Feed them all into the machine.

Press the buttons, watch the reels, follow the lights.

Feed the twenty pound note into the first machine.

Take the pound coins from the slot.

Feed them all into the other machine.

This was Robert's routine. Every day, on his way home from work, he would stop at the services and closet himself in the dark of the Game Zone. Then he would run whatever money he had through the machines. He knew that they only paid out seventy per cent of what went into them so, over time, he would lose everything, but he didn't care. It wasn't about the money.

He liked the flashing of the lights in the darkened corner of the busy services. Anyone watching would think he was oblivious to all that went on out in the brightly-lit areas behind him, but he was listening and taking it all in.

He knew when the school party arrived and spread throughout the services. He heard the arguments and endearments of couples. He heard a tray drop and the various reactions. He heard families passing on their way to and from the toilets and the shop. He heard everything and let it wash through him as his hand rose and fell from the tray to the slot and back again.

Part of him felt he shouldn't be here, that he should head straight home from work, but that was something he would only do when the money was gone. All he had there was the loneliness of a meal-for-one and every voice on the television repeating *lonely, lonely, lonely*.

No, instead he came here and fed the machines. He could be part of everything without having to join in. He could immerse himself in the bustle of the people and enjoy their journeys to distant parts.

He fed the last of the coins in his hand into the slot and spun the reels. Nothing.

He opened his wallet. Empty.

Time to go home.

He turned to leave just as another man walked into the Game Zone.

"Alright, mate," said the man. "Think I've seen you here before. How are the machines? Paying out?"

Robert ignored him and walked out into the night.

Constant Vigilance 1

REG WATCHED EVERYONE. That was his job. He needed to know where everyone was and what they were doing. And that was never more true than today.

He'd left his house mid-afternoon and walked out to his car. He'd stood by the side of it for a while, watching. Mums walked their kids home from school. Some older boys went past on bikes. Cars passed, but none slowed. A window cleaner climbed up a ladder, washed a window then climbed down again.

Only once he was sure no-one was watching him – well, not beyond the usual 'why's that guy staring at me' kind of watching – he climbed into his car and pulled away from the kerb.

His journey out of the city involved as many turns and retracings as he could manage. He watched all the time, checking out the cars around him, looking for anyone following or any signs of cars reappearing in a multiple-car hand-off.

There was nothing, so he finally powered down the slip road onto the motorway, quickly hitting a steady hundred in the outside lane, and watching for anyone attempting to keep up.

As he neared the services he waited until the very last moment before swerving across the whole carriageway to the slip lane, watching behind for anyone who tried to follow.

Nothing.

As he climbed from the car, he looked around, sizing everyone up: the door of a car at the end of his row opened and a man hurried into the services followed, more slowly, by an angry-looking woman; a coach full of school boys pulled into the far side of the car park; a young woman in a fast-food company's uniform exited from a side door and headed out towards the petrol station, a young woman in leather trousers was chased in through the doors by a man in a black cape.

He watched them all, and decided there was nothing suspicious. He patted the valuable bulge in his jacket pocket and locked the car, then walked slowly into the services and into the cafeteria.

As he walked he watched everyone around him: the angry woman now waiting outside the toilets, the man playing the fruit machines, the family heading into the shop, but no-one triggered his in-built alarm.

He walked over to the table, removed his jacket and hung it on the back of the chair, then sat down.

"Have you got it?" asked Big Tony.

"Of course," replied Reg. "Have you?"

"Stupid question. It's in the boot of the car outs −"

Big Tony was interrupted by the crash of a tray and crockery hitting the floor. Both he and Reg jerked in their seats and half-stood to look over the tables to where the noise had come from.

It was nothing, just some fool with tea on his shoes. Big Tony settled back into his seat and a moment later, after he was sure it was nothing to worry about, Reg did the same.

"So, hand it over then," said Big Tony, "and I'll take you out to it."

Reg reached for the wallet containing the money. His pocket was empty.

Closing the Circle

I T's STRANGE TO SEE yourself from another angle. I suppose famous actors have this feeling all the time. No wonder they have a distorted sense of self.

It's strange to be here. I remember this evening so well. It was the moment, the fulcrum, the single point in time which changed everything.

I didn't know that at the time, of course. And I probably would never have identified it without help, but Professor Higgins tells me he has narrowed the causality down to this single event, so here I am.

I spent some time in the dining area, drinking coffee and watching people come and go, and then, when it seemed about the right time, I got up and walked out into the main concourse area. I watched myself arrive and walk into the Game Zone and start my daily ritual of feeding the machines.

I can remember doing that, but it feels like it was someone else. Well, in the strictest sense I suppose it was. After all, this isn't my body, it's just one we've borrowed for the occasion.

I stood out in the light and watched myself in the darkness, pressing the buttons and shuttling the coins from tray to slot. I remembered how lonely and desperate I had felt. I remembered how much I had wanted to step out into the light and talk to someone, but how I hadn't. How I couldn't.

I was waiting for the event which would set me in motion, the starting gun for everything that was to come.

And finally it arrived. Someone in the cafeteria dropped a tray. It hit the floor with a loud slap and repeated hard cracks as crockery broke. I started to move closer to the Zone. I saw my younger self press the button for the last time. I watched him check his wallet and find it empty, and as he made his way back out towards his car, I walked towards him.

"Alright, mate," I said to him. "Think I've seen you here before. How are the machines? Paying out?"

He ignored me and walked out into the night, and I watched him go, but I remembered what happened next.

I remember stepping out into the night and stopping as the cold air hit me. I remembered thinking about the simple human gesture that I had just ignored. I remember deciding to finally do something different with my life, something to make it better.

And it wasn't an idle decision. As I watched my younger self leave I knew that the next day he would quit the admin job with the NHS Trust which he hated so much, and enrol at a University to take Psychology. An MSc in Neuropsychology would follow and then a PhD in mapping the mind. All that would, finally and unexpectedly, lead to the breaking of the time barrier, not for objects, but for consciousness. And all that would bring me to here, to today, to this moment, performing the action which set it all in motion.

I watch myself walk out into the night and think about all he has waiting for him: the joy of learning, the satisfaction of discovery, the love of Sanjana and, of course, little Kama.

I watch him stop just outside the doors as the moment of change passes through him and I wish him well.

Justified Violence

B IG TONY WATCHES THE tea fall, and then Reg is telling him that the money's gone; that he had the money but it's gone.

Big Tony doesn't believe Reg. Big Tony never believes anyone, especially when it comes to money or mushrooms. Everyone knows not to mention the mushrooms, but no-one quite knows why. No-one asks.

Big Tony thinks about pulling out his shooter, but there are too many bystanders, too many kiddies, too many clumsy numpties covered in tea. Instead he hauls Reg to his feet, even as Reg tries to haul his jacket on, and the two of them walk out of the building.

Big Tony heads for the far end of the car park, but there's a coach there with two boys walking towards it and what looks like a teacher following them. He pulls Reg down to the other end: to the dark, the quiet.

Big Tony asks again where the money is and Reg repeats his story. Reg had the money, in a wallet, in his jacket pocket, but now it's mysteriously gone. He'd checked he wasn't followed, he'd watched everyone on his journey, he'd had it when he sat down. "There must have been someone behind me, Tony. Someone who took it when that arse dropped his tray." No-one calls Big Tony anything other than 'Tony' to his face.

Big Tony tells Reg that he doesn't believe him. He tells him to produce the money, but Reg protests again that he can't. Reg is getting upset and scared, which seems to be something new to him. But he knows why Big Tony wants the money. Big Tony can't give the stuff to Reg without it. Big Tony is caught in a bind, running an errand for the Brothers Crumm. If he doesn't hand over this particular money to them, something bad will happen to Big Tony. And if something bad happens to Big Tony, Reg knows something bad will happen to him too.

Big Tony explains that there is honour involved. He explains that the blood on the bank notes Reg was carrying originally belonged to the eldest of the Brothers Crumm. He explains that he needs the money and that Reg needs to stop messing about. He explains this with his gun slowly forcing Reg's head back.

Big Tony hears a voice from the darkness. "Too late, Big Tony," it says.

Big Tony falls to the ground without ever hearing the shot which kills him. A second shot sounds and Reg falls on top of him. Eric Crumm fades back into the darkness.

The Pain of Frustration

A SHLEY WAS HUNGRY, he had food in front of him, but he only had one thing on his mind.

He'd steered Jodie towards the far side of the dining area, away from other people, and waited until she sat down before choosing the seat next to her, rather than the one opposite. He'd set his tray on the table and then started picking at his chips with one hand, while he rested his other on her thigh.

"How old fashioned are your parents!"

Jodie reached down and removed his hand.

"What do you mean?"

"I mean giving us separate bedrooms for the whole weekend. Okay, I know we aren't married, but we're adults, we've been going out for over two months. I mean, come *on*!"

His hand was sliding up her thigh and under her skirt. She pressed her legs together and concentrated on eating.

"It's just the way they are. They're old fashioned. I like that."

"Old fashioned is one thing, but I'm in pain!" He took her hand and attempted to place it on the front of his jeans, but she snatched it back.

"Stop it, Ashley! People might see."

He looked around. The nearest people were several tables away. "No-one will see. And what if they did? They wouldn't care. Come on, just a little stroke to keep me happy until we get back. I think my balls might explode if you don't!"

He attempted to grab her hand again, but she evaded him. His other hand was pressing higher and higher up between her thighs, almost touching her panties.

She grabbed his wrist to stop its movement and looked at him. "You know, sometimes I think you only want me for my body and for sex. You said you love me, but I'm not sure. Maybe all I am to you is a willing hole."

"Only one?" he attempted, but then seeing her face he grew serious. "Don't be silly. I think you're funny and interesting and clever and beautiful and I just love being with you. The sex we – no – the *love-making* we share is wonderful, but it's just part of what makes us a uniquely amazing couple. Of course I love you. I wouldn't say it if I didn't."

As he talked he could feel the tension in her thighs start to dissipate and he took the opportunity to slide his hand all the way up until his little finger was pressed against her warmth.

"Oh-ho!" He grinned. "And I can feel that you're not the only one who's feeling frustrated!"

She blushed and dipped her head, but her thighs opened just a little wider. He started to curl his little finger, rubbing gently against her.

When the tray of mugs hit the ground, the shock of the noise was enough to make her clamp her thighs tightly shut. The muffled crack of his little finger breaking was clearly audible, as was the gasp of pain that Ashley gave as he pulled his mangled hand free and cradled it.

Jodie looked up and around the dining area. Ashley had been right. No-one had seen, or if they had, they hadn't cared.

Constant Vigilance 2

I SEE EVERYTHING THAT goes on here. They don't think I'm paying any attention. They think I'm just the woman who scoops the fish and chips onto the scalding hot plates and thoughtlessly hands them to unsuspecting diners.

Take that Jean, for instance, she sits there, thinking she's invisible, but I know what she's up to. I can all but see her making her mental notes, copying down the facial expressions and things she overhears so she can put them in her books. She doesn't think anyone here knows who she really is, but I do. I don't say anything, though. Knowledge is power.

Margaret, the woman who comes on after her, is just as bad. She thinks no-one knows about her past, but I was here when her ex-girlfriend came in and tried to start a fight. I heard about how she broke the poor girl's heart when she ran off with another woman. But do I comment? No, I don't.

I've seen the guy in the Game Zone every time he's come in here. I've even kept count of how much money he's wasted on those machines. I don't tell anyone. Okay, so sometimes I slip over after he leaves and chance a pound. More often than not I walk away with twenty or thirty, but I don't do it every day.

I saw the fat man in the shiny suit sit down without buying anything. Waiting for a client or an accomplice in some kind of crime, I reckon. I saw the other man arrive, looking around warily, but never seeing me. I even saw the man behind him steal his wallet and walk out. I see everything that goes on here, you see.

I saw the boy in the corner sliding his hand up his girlfriend's skirt, talking her into a little public petting. I saw him get his comeuppance when the tray fell.

I saw the woman who ran into the man with the tray. I saw the man chasing the woman who ran into the man with the tray. I see everything.

And I saw young Rowan heading out to meet Julie for one of the trysts they think are so secret. Okay, so maybe it was cruel of me to make him mop up the tea, but what good is power if you don't wield a little now and again.

And a few minutes later I saw the man who stole the wallet. I saw him as I walked up to his car. I told him to hand it over or I would phone the police. He tried to argue, but he saw my knife and stopped.

I saw ten thousand pounds when I opened the wallet. That will do nicely, I thought.

The only thing I never saw was the man with the gun. The one who shot me.

I wonder if I'll see a bright light, or will it all be darkness?

The Gateway to Peril

PART 182

Our intrepid heroine, swindled-heiress and mountain-climber, Lucy Burkhampton, has finally unearthed the scroll of Sum-Dum-Gi and vanquished her evil Uncle, but as she turns to leave the cave Lord Diehardt and his guards advance, scimitars drawn. Can she fight her way past with only her trusty revolver and one solitary bullet? How can she possibly hope to win? Read on …

L UCY HELD THE GRIP of her revolver tightly in her damp grasp without a waver. The four huge guards advanced, their skin glistening from oil, their scimitars glinting in the flickering torch-light.

She took a step backwards and the stone gave beneath her feet. With a loud groan a section of the tunnel opened to the side of her and she dashed through.

This wasn't a clean escape, however, as the new passageway was short and led to a small cave lit with an unearthly light from no obvious source. In the middle was what looked like a pool of oily water, but it was upright, hanging in space, rippling in the breezes of eternity.

She didn't pause, but took a deep breath and plunged in.

But she didn't get wet. She didn't need to hold her breath at all. It wasn't liquid, but some kind of gateway.

She had passed through and now found herself some-where completely different.

She didn't stop to think but ran on, barely breaking stride, and looked around as she did so. The sky was darkening, but her surroundings – some kind of roadway leading to a brightly-lit glass building, like an exhibition centre – were bathed in a sullen orange glow. The roar of motors came from the distance.

She sped towards the building and the safety of people. As she neared she realised that what she had mistaken for sculptures were actually sleak autos, but unlike any she had seen before. They were more like spaceships than automobiles. But she had no space in her brain to wonder what kind of place would have such things, for she glanced back and saw, emerging from the oily pool behind her, not the guards, but, with cape-flying Lord Diehardt himself!

She plunged towards the building, narrowly avoiding a number of small school boys who each tried to get in her way. Her shoulder blades itched where she expected her nemesis's bullet to land at any moment, but no shot came and then she was into the lit building and amongst the people.

She glanced back. Lord Diehardt was still following. He had no cares about these innocent bystanders, he intended to take the scroll from her at all costs.

She ran on, past a dark room where a man was feeding coins into a lit box – some kind of sacrifice to a foreign god, she thought – and passed on into a dining hall.

The many different lights were disorientating, and Lucy ran straight into a man carrying a tray without even seeing him. She smelled tea in the air even as she moved on, being careful not to slip in the liquid, and then saw an open door on the far side.

She ran back out into the relief of the cold air, and skirted the building as quickly as she could, aware that Lord Diehardt was still inexorably following.

What would she do? She couldn't stay here in this foreign place. Roger was waiting for her outside the temple. She doubled-back to the place where she had come into this world and dived back through the portal.

As she stumbled out on the other side she realised why Lord Diehardt had chased her himself. The guards were waiting in a circle around the vertical pool, their four scimitars pointing at her. She stopped, unsure what to do, and moments later heard Lord Diehardt emerge behind her.

"Time to hand it over, M'Lady!" he uttered, mockingly, and she felt a fifth scimitar press into the small of her back.

Escaping from certain death by scimitar only to be faced by certain death by scimitar? Who would be so unlucky? Will our wonderful girl's luck change? Will she escape with the scroll? Will she ever see Roger again? Buy next month's issue to find out!

Extrinsic Justice

"DAMN CAT!" Eric murmured the words but saved the venom for his kick. It didn't matter, no-one was watching him. Their eyes were all on the dropped tray, the broken mugs, and the spreading pool of tea.

Eric hadn't seen the tray fall. His eyes had been fixed somewhere deeper in the cafeteria, keeping a close eye on Big Tony and Reg. He wanted to make sure everything went smoothly. He needed that money.

It wasn't about the value. This was not money he could ever spend. It was about the notes in general, and the blood which had soaked into them in particular.

The money had come from a heist. It had then, against his strict instructions, been paid out to a 'contractor' for services rendered. The person to blame had been dealt with, as had the contractor, but the money hadn't been found. So the word had been spread that Eric needed this particular wad of cash returned to him.

Of course no-one was willing to simply hand it over, so deals had had to be done. That was all normal. And now Eric wanted to make sure that Big Tony carried it all out correctly. He was already on his last warning.

A myth had grown up around the money, something about 'honour', but the truth was far more prosaic. The notes were marked, the serial numbers were registered, and the blood which stained them came both from Eric and from the policeman he'd killed when he stole it.

He needed to get the money and he needed to burn the money and he needed for no-one to know the real reason he needed it. If the truth got out then someone with a grudge would finally have what they needed to bring Eric down.

There were plenty of people with grudges out there.

Eric really needed that money.

So it was with horror that, as the sound of the breaking mugs was still fresh in his ears, he saw some young scrote reach over and lift a bulging wallet from Reg's pocket then walk out.

He didn't wait for the revelation of the theft to hit the lackeys, he followed the thief instead, only pausing to frighten the cat which tried to trip him.

Out in the car park he watched as the thief made his way to a car. He watched as a waitress approached the man. He waited, his fingers running over the trigger-guard of the gun in his pocket.

When the conversation between the two came to an end the woman walked away with the wallet in her hands. Eric waited until she was in the shadows, approaching the rear door of the building, then he stepped up, placed the end of the silencer against the rear of her skull and pulled the trigger.

He leaned down and scooped up the wallet from her lifeless fingers, then checked the contents. It was all there. Good.

He turned back towards the front of the building in time to see Big Tony and Reg exit and walk out to the far side of the car park. He followed and, in swift order, dealt with them too.

Satisfied that the job was done, Eric stepped around the blood on the tarmac and walked towards his car.

From out of the dark, a voice said, "Excuse me?"

Eric turned and was engulfed in a bright light. The next thing he saw was like a scene from a science fiction film: a metallic room, panels with flashing lights and read-outs, a giant screen showing Earth from orbit. He shook his head, in part to clear what was obviously a hallucination, in part to negate something which seemed all too real.

"I really couldn't leave you down there." It was the man from the car park. Eric remembered seeing him in the restaurant while he had been waiting for Reg to show up. Eric had thought the man looked strange. Now, with his hat removed to display a fine layer of tentacles where hair should have been, he looked all the stranger.

"I don't normally do this – I only popped in for a cup of tea and toasted teacake – but you really had to be stopped. In all my travels you have to be one of the most heartless and evil men I have ever come across." The man held up a strange-looking instrument with a long finger-like spike of metal pointing towards Eric.

Still confused and unsure what was happening, Eric shook his head again. "Is that ..." He paused and licked his lips which were dry. "Is that an anal probe?"

"What is it with you people and anal probes?" asked the alien. "Why does everyone ask if this is an anal probe?"

The outsider looked questioningly at Eric who said nothing.

"Well, as a matter of fact, this one *is* an anal probe. But that's beside the point!" His grin was unpleasant as he advanced on Eric

Thirty seconds later the screaming started. It went on for a very long time.

A Story of More Woe

JULIE HEARD THE tray drop but she kept going. She didn't want to be grabbed for clean-up duty. She took her usual route out through the rear door and out into the car park.

Why do I do this? she wondered, as she did nearly every day. After all, she was a good modern feminist. She needed a man like a fish needed an iPod, or whatever. So why did she feel the need to make this trip every day, to slip – onlookers permitting – into Rowan's slightly greasy embrace and feel the traces of his acne rub on her cheeks? Why couldn't she tell him 'no' and end it, as she wanted to? Was she really so weak? Was she really so empty?

She reached the shelter and found it empty. No onlookers, but also no Rowan.

So, she waited.

And waited.

She knew what had happened, of course. That nosy Barbara had always had it in for the pair of them. She would have cornered Rowan and made him mop up the tea. That was where he was: mopping when he should have been kissing her. For God's sake, could he not be more of a man? If she was going to do this ... this ... *thing* every day, then the least he could be was a proper bloke. But no, he was a wimpy, easy-to-push-over, never-say-no kind of guy who would let anyone with a loud enough voice stamp all over him.

Well, that was definitely it. She wasn't going to put up

with it anymore. She was going to end it, call it off, find a real man.

She waited.

And waited.

Maybe he would get it done quickly and still have time to nip out and see her. Maybe he cared about her enough to put his back into it and work hard so he could snatch a moment with her. Maybe he could show that he really meant it when he said he loved her by turning up, even if only for a single peck.

But no, that much effort was beyond him. He was a typical bloke. Anything like hard work was too much trouble for him. There was no way he was ever going to put himself out for her. She should end it, call it off, find herself someone better.

She checked her watch, sighed, and started to walk back.

As she neared the door it opened in front of her, spilling light into the car park. Rowan stepped out carrying a bucket of murky water. He set it beside the door then looked up and saw her.

The smile he gave her made her heart take flight. Butterflies played kiss-chase in her stomach and she wanted nothing more than to feel his warm, safe hands hold her and his succulent lips pressing against hers.

That was when the door swung open wide enough for the light to reveal Barbara's body lying on the tarmac between them.

Julie screamed and the world turned grey. Rowan took two strides, leapt over the body and caught Julie before her buckled legs could drop her to the ground. He scooped her up and carried her back inside. He laid her gently on one of the chairs in the staff room, then pulled out his phone to call the police.

Immanence

VERONICA WAITED IN the queue, a cup of coffee and a slice of cheesecake balanced on her tray, and pondered once again the possible ways she could kill herself.

These were thoughts which had been growing in her mind over the last few weeks, and now were almost a constant presence.

It didn't distress her to find her head full of such thoughts, though she was careful not to mention it to anyone because she knew they wouldn't feel so calm. They were comforting thoughts, in a way.

It wasn't even that she was particularly depressed, or stressed. She had just calmly and rationally come to the decision that the world would be better off without her, and she wouldn't have to carry on with an existence which was, in the end, if she was honest, pointless.

The only thing preventing her was that most of the ways people killed themselves either seemed quite painful, or weren't foolproof. She had no desire at all to be paralysed or brain-damaged or even inconvenienced too much. An off switch would be the best thing, she'd thought the other night. She'd laughed aloud when she'd thought that, her laughter sounding strange in the empty flat. She didn't laugh very often, she realised.

She looked around her: at the back of the man in front of her in the queue, and the dithery woman in front of him; at the couples and families dotted around the restaurant, at the various people waiting for others. She wondered what they were thinking about and what they would make of her thoughts if she spoke them aloud.

A commotion near the doors caught her attention. A young woman in leather trousers and a rough blue shirt ran in. She was being chased by a man in a long black cape. Veronica presumed it was a stunt of some kind, perhaps an advert for a new chocolate bar.

The woman headed almost directly for Veronica, just missing her and colliding with the man in front of her instead. His tray tumbled from his hands, hitting the floor with a slap. Hot tea leapt from broken mugs and splattered up the front of her legs, soaking quickly through her tights and onto her legs.

She hopped back out of the way, careful not drop her own tray, and winced at the pain of the scald. It was only momentary – she hadn't got an awful lot of tea on her, and it was cooling quickly – but it had been enough to startle and shake her.

She looked up from her legs to see the man who had dropped the tray looking at her. Of the woman and the man in the cape, there was no sign.

"Are you alright?" asked the man from the queue.

Veronica looked at him. He looked strange. In fact, the whole room did. It was all more alive, more vibrant, more *there* than it had been a few moments before. It was as though the pain of the hot tea on her legs had woken her from a dream. She felt something shift inside her.

The man stepped closer, his loafers sloshing through tea, and Veronica vaguely heard a woman calling for a mop and bucket. "Are you okay?" asked the man.

Veronica felt tears running down cheeks bulging from a smile which stretched her lips. She nodded. "Yes. I am. Thank you. I'm fine."

Undercover Surveillance

DETECTIVE SERGEANT TOM Michaels was blessed with a young-looking face. Well, maybe 'blessed' was the wrong word. Sometimes 'cursed' would have been better.

He was nearly thirty-four, but could easily pass for nineteen; seventeen in poor light. As a result he got all the jobs which needed someone to go undercover in a 'young' occupation. He'd flipped burgers and asked if people wanted fries; he'd occasionally served behind bars, but more often found himself collecting glasses, and now he was working in a motorway service station selling papers, drinks, chocolate and cigarettes to hordes of travellers.

He was just glad this wasn't his main job. He would have gone crazy.

His assignment this time, as every time, was to watch out for the bad guys. There had been intelligence received that this services was being used for exchanges. No-one quite knew what was being exchanged yet, but they knew it was Crumm and his boys, and they knew that something was going down tonight.

So Michaels had been crow-barred onto the staff roster at the beginning of the week, just in case the villains were staking out the place, and had bided his time.

He'd finally seen Crumm come in earlier and take up a vantage point in the dining area.

A little later he'd seen Big Tony arrive, closely followed by Reg Smith.

The latter two had settled down to talk, seemingly unaware of Crumm's surveillance.

And through it all, Michaels kept a surreptitious watch.

When a tray hit the floor of the dining area, he flinched and looked over. For a split-second he'd thought it was a shot being fired. He saw movement to his left and in the overhead mirror caught sight of first two schoolboys and then a middle-aged man filling their pockets with chocolate. It was a flagrant crime, but Michaels didn't care. His eyes were on Crumm and his associates.

Crumm was already moving, ignoring the scene which seemed to be developing between Reg and Big Tony, and heading for the doors. A few moments later, his two colleagues stood up as well, though whether they were following or whether it was a coincidence, Michaels couldn't tell.

The undercover cop called over the other assistant – Melanie? Mandy? Michaela? – and told her he had to take a toilet break, then walked out after his prey. If he was quick he could catch them in the middle of the exchange of whatever it was.

When he stepped out of the building, they were nowhere to be seen. He wasted some valuable time heading towards the petrol station, following someone who turned out not to be Crumm. As he headed back towards the lonely end of the car park, Crumm came out of the dark in front of him, alone. Then a strange-looking man stepped out of the shadows behind him. Michaels thought maybe he'd seen the guy in the restaurant, but couldn't be sure.

"Excuse me?" said the guy.

Crumm span round, there was a bright flash of light, and then Crumm was gone.

As his eyesight returned, Michaels saw that the man was still there and was holding a strange metallic gun in his hand, pointing it at the tarmac. He tipped his hat and Michaels saw a layer of pinkish tentacles where his hair should have been. The man then turned aside and indicated the bodies of Reg and Big Tony, one on top of the other.

Michaels stared at the man for a moment and nodded, one law enforcement officer to another, and the strange man disappeared.

That was when he heard a scream from the back of the main building. He turned and ran towards it, already suspecting what he might find. This was going to be a long night.

Hot and Cold

JOE TURNED AWAY FROM the counter with his Oreo Krushem already chilling his hand, just in time to see his dad drop a tray full of tea on the floor.

For a moment, Joe thought about going over to help clean up and to fetch new teas. After all, he was a grown-up, nearly thirty, and that was the proper responsible thing to do. But part of him was still fifteen and just couldn't quite be arsed.

And, besides, Joe wasn't really that interested in his dad's latest mishap. They were par for the course. Instead his attention was on the woman who had been behind his dad in the queue. She was beautiful, and looked seriously sexy in a dark business suit and heels. Joe had noticed her flinch when the tray was dropped. It might have been just the noise, but she might also have been splashed with hot tea.

She hadn't seemed bothered – in fact her face had brightened into the smile which had drawn Joe's attention – and his dad had been solicitous enough, but Joe still reckoned that another apology was in order and would definitely give him an 'in'.

So he watched as she went and sat down and then went over to help his dad.

He put his milkshake onto the tray and lifted it from his dad's hands, then carried it over and placed it on a table in full view of the woman. When his mum and dad, Uncle

Jim and Aunt Maureen had caught up and sat down, Joe took his milkshake off the tray, said, "Back in a minute," and headed over to the woman's table.

She was already watching him as he walked over, the remains of that smile still on her lips.

"Hi there," he said, giving her a smile of his own.

"Hi."

"I just thought I'd come over and apologise for my dad."

She looked surprised and Joe thought he saw the remains of tears on her face. "Really? Well, that's very kind of you, but there's really no harm. I just got a little splashed. It'll dry out soon enough."

"Splashed? Were you burned?" he glanced down at her legs, but not long enough to be creepy.

"No, not at all. I'm fine, really. In fact, I think he did me a favour."

This was unexpected, and Joe took this as an invitation to have a fuller conversation. He indicated the chair opposite her and, when she nodded, he sat down, placing the iced milkshake on the table in front of him. "I'm Joe, by the way," he said, holding out his hand.

"Veronica." Her hand was warm and dry and had a good grip. Joe was careful not to hold on for too long.

"So," he said, picking up the thread, "a favour?"

Veronica looked at him steadily for a moment, and he felt uncomfortable and a little exposed, as though she was looking right into him. Then she laughed and the feeling faded.

"I'm sorry. I just realised I have no idea who you are and I was about to tell you something I've never told anyone."

He shrugged. "Why not? Maybe a stranger is the best person to tell. Fewer repercussions that way." He smiled then suddenly gave a mock-frown. "You haven't killed anyone, have you?"

She looked shocked, and blushed, and for a moment Joe was really quite concerned that he'd guessed correctly, but then she laughed again. "No. Not yet. But, well, when your dad dropped his tray and I got splashed, I was thinking about killing myself."

She said it so matter-of-factly that Joe knew she wasn't joking. He felt a shiver go down his spine, but also felt his attraction for this woman start to turn into something else. He found he wanted to hold her and tell her not to worry, that it would all be alright, that he was here for her.

"Really?"

"Yes." Now she was talking it seemed as though a dam had burst and more words poured from her. "I've been thinking about it for a while. I sit in my rented flat with no partner, no family, no pets – not allowed them in the flat, you see – and only my job to keep my warm, and I wonder what good I'm doing in the world."

Joe wanted to say something but was worried that anything he did say would sound trite. He opened his mouth to try anyway, but she waved him to silence.

"Don't worry. I know how self-pitying and stupid that is. It's giving up before you've really tried. I've never bought a house, not because I can't afford it – I'm a solicitor and, if you don't mind me saying so, a damn good one – but because I thought that was something you did with your partner. But why should I wait? I could buy one now, then I could get a cat or a dog or, I don't know, a python or something! And then I could maybe go out more, try to meet someone. And, 'Why don't you come back to my house,' sounds far better than, 'Fancy climbing four flights of stairs to my bedsit,' don't you think?"

Joe nodded and didn't even try to speak. He needed to let this run its course.

"And I could work a little less. Work only fills my life because I let it. If I decided to do other things – Salsa dancing, for instance, I've always fancied that – then I would have to make time for it. And you know what made me realise all that?"

The question took Joe by surprise and he had barely stammered, "No. What?" before she was off again.

"It was the feeling of hot tea hitting my legs. It did hurt, yes, I won't deny it, but it only lasted a moment. I would never dream of dropping hot tea on myself, I'd be afraid of the pain, just as I'm afraid of every fucking thing – 'scuse my language – in life. So if I can put up with that, I can put up with anything, so I should wake up, shut up whining, and get out there and do something about it all."

Joe was gaping by this point. He finally pulled his mouth shut and asked, "All that from a few drops of tea?"

She laughed and he laughed with her. She reached out and put her warm hand on his, cold from where his drink had chilled it. "Yes," she said, "all that from a few drops of tea."

Joe was about to say what he hoped was the right thing when they heard a scream from behind the kitchens. The room went silent then filled with the sound of chairs scraping as people stood to look. A few moments later the young man in the Burger King uniform who had mopped up the spilled tea earlier came running in from the back.

"Somebody's shot Barbara!" he screamed, then pressed his phone to his ear and turned away.

Joe felt Veronica's hand tighten over his and he turned back to her. He didn't pause to calculate his words, they just came out of his mouth: "Don't worry, it'll be alright. I'm here."

You Caught My Eye

I LIKE TO SIT and people-watch. It gives me the chance to wonder who these people are, who they love and who loves them. It gives me the chance to wonder what's going on in their heads.

I like train stations, they're good: lots of people coming and going, journeys starting and ending and each one a new adventure.

A&E waiting rooms work too: all those people with stories to tell of nights out and heavy drinking, of brave battles with chronic illnesses, of attempts to see which strange objects they can lodge in their rectums.

But my favourites are motorway service stations. That chance to see people mid-journey, mid-adventure. It's intoxicating.

Okay, yes, there are staff there too, fixed and immobile. But I never bother with them. They're just the garnish to the rest of the travelling human buffet: the customers. They come in all shapes and sizes, and I can sit and pick through them at my leisure.

I like women travelling alone. They never fail to surprise, either with how easy they are to snare, or how much they fight once you've got them. Lone truck drivers are interesting, but never quite as hard as you would expect. If all else fails there are always the hitchhikers. But they're like fast food: too easy to get hold off, too quick to pass, and you always want another after half an hour.

Today's crop are prize-pickings. There seem to be so many interesting people in here that I don't know who to choose. Whose brain is going to look good in a jar on my shelf?

I ponder, as I have before, the man who fritters his money on the fruit machines. But that feels even easier than a hitchhiker.

There's one of those here, too. You can always tell them apart. Not quite as clean as they think they are, and a certain desperation in the eyes.

Who to choose? Who to choose?

And then my choice is made for me. A loud noise draws my attention and there he is, presiding over broken crockey and a pool of tea. His ill-fitting suit and the gorm-less expression on his face make him ripe for my shelf. I notice he has people with him, another man, a couple of women and … yes, that young man over by KFC. His son? Who knows.

I normally like them alone, but I think he'll do. There's just something about the way the whole building seems to revolve around him and his dropped tray that shines a special light on him. He's the only one that will do for me now.

I'll probably have to follow them home to wherever they live. This might be one of my extended campaigns. I've not done one of those for a while. But, eventually, if I watch him long enough, he'll be all on his own. And then he's mine.

I throw him a little nod, not to draw his attention, simply to mark him.

You're it, my friend, I tell him. You caught my eye.

The Centre Cannot Hold
(a Simple Tray)

– You got the teas then, Bob.

– I did, Though I could murder a pint.

– Me too. When we get back, aye?

– Aye. You're on.

– Splendid.

– The ladies still in the loo?

– Yeah, you know what they're like.

– I do, Jim, I do.

– Where's your Joe?

– Off getting one of those fancy fried–chicken milk-shakes.

– A what?

– Them KFC people, they do fancy milkshakes with biscuits and stuff in them.

– How do you suck a biscuit up a straw?

– That's what I asked him.

– What did he say?

– Slowly.

– Fair dos, Bob. Fair dos.

– Oh, here come the ladies, Jim.

– That's not all, Bob. Watch out!

– Shit! Fuck! Where did she come from?

– Out of nowhere, mate. She just popped up.

– Damn. Look out everyone, there's a spreading tide of tea!

– Nicely put, Bob. Here, use these napkins. You got some on you.

– Thanks. Oh, bugger, are you alright, miss? I'm so sorry.

– Give her some of your napkins, Bob.

– Are you okay, miss?

– Leave her be, Bob, you'll creep her out.

– Oh, watch out, here comes the guy with the mop.

– Saving your bacon, Bob.

– Mopping my tea, Jim, mopping my tea.

– Four more cups, then?

– Aye. Good plan. Good plan. Then we can all forget about this and pretend it never happened.

– I don't think it was a major event in anyone else's life, Bob. No need to worry.

Intervention

As the police took statement after statement, the author sat in the middle of the maelstrom and considered what he'd created. This wasn't quite what he'd envisaged all those months ago, in the pub, with Ross.

"What you should do," said Ross, "is you should set all of the stories in a single place at a single time. Use one event to tie them all together."

"Ooh, nice," said the author. "Like a motorway service station and something happens."

"Someone could drop a tray," said Mike, who was there too.

"Yes. Yes! I like it," said the author.

But did he still like it? Dead bodies piling up in the car park, at least one broken bone, mounds of stolen confectionary and Bob, one of his favourite recurring characters, besmirched with tea: was this really what he'd wanted when he'd started?

He thought about winding backwards through it all. Send the police home, cancel Rowan's phone call, silence Julie's scream, bring Eric back from his close encounter, breathe life back into Barbara and Reg and Big Tony. Is that what he should do? He could un-break Ashley's finger and put the toilet paper back on the rolls.

If he went back and found another way out for Lucy – he wasn't worried about that, she *always* found a way out – then he could stop the tray from ever getting dropped.

If he did that he could save Bob's trousers and everything else that unfolded.

But did he have the right? If he did that, Joe wouldn't have an 'in' with Veronica and she might go through with her sad and desperate plan.

Robert might never leave his fruit-machine coma and find happiness.

And, most importantly, that bastard Crumm wouldn't get his comeuppance.

No, decided the author. It was too much. The deed was done and he would have to live with it.

He looked around, and wondered if there was anything, any little thing, that he could do to make amends, any Afterwords he could craft.

He wound back and forth through the stories. What could he do?

He stopped off in the staff room to convince Julie that Rowan really was the one, and she should stop worrying. It wasn't easy but it was worth it.

He gave Ashley a couple of wooden stirrers from the coffee station and a rubber band from his pocket to splint his finger, that should do until they got to A&E.

Was that enough, wasn't there something else?

Oh.

Yes.

He wandered outside, unnoticed by the police and all the other witnesses because that was what he wanted. He walked through the darkness to a silver Mondeo, and he waited.

As the police started releasing the various travellers, the man he was waiting for emerged from the building and walked across the tarmac towards the author who turned and pretended to fiddle with the lock of the adjacent car.

The author listened as the footsteps slowed and stopped. The man was close, but not close enough.

"Is there a problem?" asked the man. The author mumbled something in response.

"Pardon?" asked the man.

The author mumbled again, and the man took the last precious step.

The author turned and sank his knife into the belly of the serial killer. He held it there, as the man gasped, then jerked it free. The man dropped to the tarmac, taking in erratic, wheezing breaths.

The author bent down, bringing his face close to his dying character. "Leave. Bob. Alone," he said then straightened up and walked back out of the story.